Table of Contents

MW00961492

1

Deep In the Woods

Sam and Duke are two brothers that have
been hunting vampires and monsters longer than
they would care to remember. Their parents were a
happy couple that raised them on the cost of
Monterey. Where they could enjoy nature and the
city whenever they chose. Till one day a pack of
blood thirsty vampires came to town, leaving body
trails wherever they went. While their parents Niyah
and Reed were on their way for a fun drive up the
coast on warm and sunny day, they encountered the
vampires at a gas station. They were hungry thugs
that picked people off at will and quite randomly.
After Niyah and Reed filled up the gas tank and
purchased a couple of snacks for the trip, they
continued on their drive. However, through the
joyful time they were completely clueless to fact
that they were being followed. Soon they pulled
over to take in the beautiful beach scenery and snap
a few pictures. However, their fun was soon
interrupted as the gang of vampires pulled over and
got out of their cars. Reed could smell trouble and
he was about to head back to the car but he was
quickly rushed. He gave them a strong fight, sucker
punching one and hitting two in the gut. But they
recovered pretty quickly and before he knew it
Niyah was bitten and dragged to the ground. He
screamed in rage and tried to get them off, but it
was too late. The rough and savage vampires
tackled him and knocked him out cold, as his body

laid cold and shivering at the beachside. Once he came to, he found Niyah missing! He felt his heart sink into his stomach and his heart beat so fast that he could hardly breathe. He quickly rushed into the car and drove up and down the beach, but found no site of his beloved wife Niyah. Now confused, disoriented and hungry, he pulled into the same gas station as earlier. Reed cleaned up, flashed a photo of Niyah to the gas attendant asking if he saw his wife, but the attendant hadn't seen her. Reed was heartbroken; he went to the police station to report the crime. He explained all of the details and how they were attacked while trying to take photos of the coast. He said, "Even though I know it sounds unbelievable, but I am sure that they bit her as if they were animals." The police officer taking his statement told him they'd do everything to find her. He had another officer contact the gas station for video footage, and luckily enough the attendant was able to send everything via computer. Yet they still had no solid evidence to go on, other than a grainy video image from the gas station.   This meant the case would be terribly hard to solve and the trail was already getting cold.

      With that Reed decided he had to drive back home to tell the boys now 16 and 18 that their mother was missing and likely terribly hurt. When he arrived home the boys could tell just by looking at their dad that something was awfully wrong. Sam was the first to speak up asking, "What's wrong, where's mom?" Reed explained everything and said that he's going to do everything in his power to find their mother. And so he did, he spent many years trying to find her. After some time he came to terms with the fact the attackers were indeed vampires,

3

even though he never believed such things truly existed in real life. Yet he accepted it, he did all the research he could to learn about them and where they hid out. He drove city to city looking for the same thugs. When he finally found them he learned that Niyah was bled to death. This completely devastated Reed and he was never able to find her body for a proper burial. But he got his vengeance by slaying each and every one of the vampires involved and burnt their bodies to a crisp. Afterwards, he vowed to hunt every vampire he could find to prevent such a thing happening to anyone else. Over time he became an expert, teaching Duke what he could along the way. Reed angrily searched throughout the state for vampires, staking and decapitating any and every vampire in his path. Until he met his match and was killed. That's when Duke and Sam stepped in to continue their dad's mission. Sam is two years younger than Duke and has always looked up to his older brother for advice in life and hunting skills. They both do what they do to rid the world of vicious monsters that love to prey on unsuspecting people. Yet both have different ways of hunting, Duke has more of a temper and is ready for a fight till death. While Sam likes to appraise situations first and if there's a cure he's all for finding one.

Meanwhile, Placerville is a beautiful town surrounded by woods and is enjoyed by both locals and tourists. It's late in the afternoon, the air is fresh and crisp, perfect for a stroll. Alex is running in the woods and looking behind him for it. He gathers a few rocks hoping that he can stop it. Then he tries to steady his breathing and hides.

The sound of it zipping through the woods is loud and scary. Alex tries to compose himself but it lands nearby and it's getting closer. Currently, Duke and Sam are sitting in their spiffy black skylark reading the papers and discussing the next case. Sam says "Not much is going on" and can't decide what job to pick up. While discussing, they notice an extremely large birdlike object fly by! Duke almost drops his cup of coffee and asks "Whoa what was that?" It moved by so swiftly they could hear the wind passing from its large dark wings. They felt excited and are sure it was something worth checking out. They exit the car go to the trunk and pull out a couple of guns and cross the road into the forest where they follow the birdlike creature. They hide behind a tree and can now see it standing. What they see is completely surprising, it's very large and dark with sharp piercing eyes. There is a look of hunger apparent on its face as it comes closes towards Alex. His chance of escape is minimal. Duke whispers to Sam quietly to follow his lead as they lean against a tree for coverage. Next they spread out so that they are on two sides of the tree. Duke questions if they're looking at a bat. Sam takes a long look and says "I think it is but I've never seen one that large." They stare at its large featherless black wings that practically touch the forest floor.

Duke decides to shoot now and ask questions later, there's no time for delay. They move in closer to get a better shot, but Sam steps on a small twig that breaks loud enough for bat ears. At this very moment it turns directly towards them wondering who's coming but it turns its hungry face back towards Alex. Who's been waiting for the right time to toss them into its face. He throws a handful of rocks with all of his strength at the bat, since he couldn't find anything else. Unfortunately, it starts coming closer, now Alex is completely scared, he feels a large lump in his throat and he can hardly think, the bat smells awful and he can almost feel it's breath beating down on him. Alex has only one option to run, so he does bolting further into the woods moving swiftly like a deer running from its hunter. Worried that they're going to lose someone, Duke takes a shot at the bat but it doesn't kill it, instead it lets out a sharp razor like scream and flies off. They try to shoot again but it's now completely out of sight. Sam wonders how was it able to move that fast, he doesn't know if the shot will stop it in mid-flight and force it to land, but he and Duke run toward Alex. Who now stops to catch his breath, and take it all in. I am sure that I heard gun shots thinks Alex as he sees two armed men nearing him. Sam and Duke asks if Alex is okay. Still panting and out of breath, he says "Yeah, it didn't touch me, what was that thing, a bat?" Duke looks puzzled and repeats the question with a confused stare and says "We're sure it's a bat." In any case Alex tells them it was awful and begins to tell what happened "I was going for a run, then all of a sudden I saw something large hovering over me, then it began circling after me. Once I became sure I started running, but then it began coming closer. "Thanks for everything, if you guys hadn't come in time, it would have killed me for sure." He introduces himself to Duke and Sam. They shake hands while offering him a comforting pat on the back. "Hey, no problem, we're glad we were here to help," says Sam. "Yeah no problem Alex I am glad that we

could help," says Duke. He asks where Alex's
headed and if wants a lift? Alex says, "Yeah, sure I
am going back home which is a further up the main
road." Duke tells Alex to come along, the car isn't
far away. He then explains that he and Sam are
hunters passing through. He points out their shiny,
sleek and raven like skylark parked near the road.
Alex's impressed by the car and asks if Duke's a bit
of a car buff, which makes them both laugh. Duke
says, "You could say that, it was handed down from
our father, so we take good care of it." They arrive
at the car, climb in and head towards Alex's home.
As they drive Duke explains that they are looking
for game to hunt till they saw something large
moving through the trees. He asks Alex if he's seen
it before. Alex says no, he's been in town for about
a year and it's pretty nice and calm. He says "I've
never seen or heard of anything like it before." Alex
talks about how he's gone out for deer hunts with
friends and it had always been pretty peaceful. He
wonders aloud what happens if those gunshots don't
kill the bat, it might go back into the woods and
make it a hunting ground.   Sam says, "I've been
thinking about it to, we probably didn't kill it but
maybe the authorities can." Duke agrees and adds
"Yeah we'll stay on this one and report it to the
ranger, so they can keep an eye out for it." Adding
it would be best to stay out of the woods and warn
others to do the same until you know for sure the
thing is dead or captured." Alex says "You bet, I am
definitely going to let everyone know about this,
I've never seen something that big or strong you
saw how easily it took those shots." As they arrive
at Alex's home it looks very nice, with blue paint
and large windows. It fits in well with the

surroundings. Alex is happy to arrive safe and sound. He says, "Thanks a lot guys, I owe you, would you guys like to come in for a bite to eat?" They politely decline. Sam says, "We can't stay because we're going to try and track down this bat before it actually kills someone." Alex nods and tells them that they are welcome anytime. Adding that he will report what happened to the ranger and hopes they can capture it. Duke says, "Sounds good, take care of yourself and try to keep out of the woods till the area is clear." They exchange goodbyes, as Alex heads indoors relived to be home safe and sound. Duke and Sam walk away from the door and look back at the house admiring its quaint beauty and tranquility. When they return to the car Duke turns on the radio to see if there is anything on about the bat they saw earlier. As he is scanning through Sam hears an announcement come in and stops scanning. There's a complaint about a large dark birdlike thing near a window further in town. When they arrive the police are already there, the front lawn is cornered off with yellow crime scene tape and broken glass lay on the beautifully trimmed front lawn. The police are finishing up. Duke walks over to the officer, flashes a convincing fake badge and says he's with the FBI and wants a few details. The cop explains that someone reported a large bird near here, but upon arrival only found broken glass at the house. So they knocked on the door, heard shouts for help and found the victim along with his family inside. The officer informs them that the father was bit, so an ambulance took the victim to the local hospital. Duke thanks him for the information and says, "We'll head over to the hospital for more details." He then walks back to the car and tells Sam that from what the cop told him it sounds like the bat they saw in the woods attacked the father. Both are thankful the kids were not hurt. Duke says the father's at the hospital getting treatment for a bite wound. Sam's surprised and says that they should head to the hospital and get the rest of the story. Sam starts to wonder about just what kind of bat they are dealing with.

They head off to the hospital, it's early in the evening; the waiting area is full. One person is sitting hovelled over and moaning with pain as his family comforts him. Others are waiting and checking their smart phones as hospital staff move to from with urgency. Sam and Duke take in the scene as they walk up to the nursing station looking for the victim. She directs them over to room thirteen. They see the victim lying still in bed with a bandage wrapped around his neck. They knock before entering to get his attention, and then walk over and introduce themselves. Sam says, "Hi we're with the FBI and wanted to get a statement on what happened to you." The victim states his name is James, and begins to describe what happened. Despite everything James is very positive, yet truly exhausted after his ordeal. He explains that it started in the evening when he was lying down in his bedroom tired from work. The rooms was warm so he opened the bedroom window for some air. Then he laid down and soon feel asleep. He says, "During my sleep, I thought that I was having a nightmare, I was sweating and struggling a bit." However, he was awaken by the feel of sharp fangs entering his neck.

2

It's In the Town

James says, "He knows that it was real, he felt the
pain all the way through his neck, and it was like
nothing I've ever experienced. I tried to hit at him
and push him but he was too strong but I kept on."
He thinks one of his neighbors must have heard the
commotion and called the police. When they kicked
open the door only then did the man turn and run
away towards the window. When the police entered
he told them everything, and they saw the bite and
blood. They said perhaps it was a rabid dog that
came in from the cat door and not the man hovering
over him. "I am sure it's was a man but the police
stated that I could have been half asleep. There was
blood all over my bed," exclaims James.   He adds,
"I am sure about what I saw even though it doesn't
make sense, because how could a man chew at my
neck? If the police hadn't come I think this monster
would've chewed my neck off completely." Sam
says, "I am glad they came when they did. But can I
ask you, did you get a good enough look at him to
describe him?" James tells them he got a good luck
at it "It was dark but his eyes were sort of yellow
and he had dark slicked hair. He was wearing all
black. Also he or it was very strong and tall." Duke
asks did the attacker take or say anything.
James says, "No, like I said at first I was asleep, it
took off after the police shot at it. But I didn't notice
any blood from it and it didn't seem phased by the
bullets. I am sure the cops didn't miss". Sam looks
James straight in the eyes, places a hand on his

shoulder adding, "Well, we're going to do our best to solve the case." Duke says, "I think that we have all the information that we need to follow up on, just get some rest and the police will look out for this guy." James says "Okay and thanks so much for coming." He turns to get some rest, as they rise up to leave. Duke reminds him to get some rest and the nurses will take care of him. James is hopeful as he turns to his side and shuts his eyes. Out in the hall Duke and Sam discuss what's going on so far. Duke says, "So I am thinking we have a vampire out on the loose, you think it's coming back for him, since he didn't kill him." Sam replies "Who knows, but we can keep tabs on him, besides when he starts to change he'll be dangerous." Duke agrees and explains that they need to find out the bat's hideout and if they're more like it. Sam thinks if it's the bat they saw in woods, it will be a flying vampire, and very hard to catch, but not impossible.

However there's something else that needs to be settled with James, Duke says, "Now we've got to turn James back before he feeds and turns into a bloodsucker, otherwise we'll have to kill him." Sam doesn't think killing James at the hospital will work because there are too many people around but they can wait until he's released. They hope the hospital will give him something to keep him asleep till they can get him the cure. "Let's hope so, for now we've got to get the leader, but where is he?" asks Duke.

Sam feels hungry and says, "Let's get a bite to eat, find the layer and go back to the hospital tonight and give James the cure to stop him from changing into a vampire." "Sounds good, let's get out of here," says Duke. All the while they are unaware that they are being followed by the very

11

vampire they're trying to kill. Duke and Sam head out and get into the car. The Vampire is now in his man form, wearing a dark navy blue suit and gets into his grey sports car. Duke says, "It's risky leaving that guy in the hospital, but I don't think we can convince him to take the concoction, no questions asked." Sam agrees, "Maybe we can try to explain later and let him decide for himself." Soon they arrive at a nice little diner in a quiet place in town. It's nice in the inside, there's a long shiny red counter and plenty of cushiony booths. Sam and Duke choose a booth out of the way. The waiter comes and they place an order. They both have cheeseburgers, fries and a soda. They get started with their computer search. Duke says, "You know so far this is the first flying vampire that we've had to catch, I thought they only existed in movies. After dinner, I say we go back to the hospital before he comes back for James." Sam agrees, "Maybe we should let him take James, then track them to his layer and attack them from that point." Duke thinks that it could work but they will have to try to put some space between them and the vampire because it may have picked up on their scents from the woods, and like a dog he can smell and track them from far away. Sam knows he is right and tells Duke that they will have to be very careful at the hospital as well so no one gets hurt. Once the food arrives everything looks and smells perfect, and they are excited to get a warm meal. Soon they begin to eat and enjoy every bite.

Duke wants to take a break from plotting and planning for just a moment and says, "Since we've gotten many monsters and ghouls off our to do list. Have you started to think about going back to school?" Sam says, "That kind of sounds like a good idea, I've been thinking that we need a little change, plus it's been awhile since we had any normalcy in our lives." "Well we've been too busy to think about it, but a simple, happy life would suit me just fine after everything," exclaims Duke. They've been busy for years hunting bad guys, that they've almost forgotten their promise to live a normal life. Sam says, "It's great to be hunters and get these bad guys out of here, but a part of me would like to see what else life has to offer." He wonders can he devout some of his time to himself, and his mind often goes back to the subject only to be faced with another interruption.   Duke completely understands and sees the potential that Sam has, he's a great researcher and certainly could use his talents for a scholarly purpose. He says, "I am proud of you little brother and I think you deserve a better life, it's something that I know for sure Mom and Dad would've wanted." Sam thinks maybe its possible and wants to give it a shot soon. Duke says, "But for now we've got to get this vampire/bat, it was huge. With that thing lose these people don't stand a chance." Sam says, "Well we know it's got to be a vampire, so that means we already know how to kill it. The only question is where is it? And are there more, because being able to fly will make it a whole lot harder to catch." They finish up their meal while researching about vampire bats and how to kill them. This will be the first time they've killed such a thing, the thought is exciting for the young hunters. While they talk, the vampire enters the diner, sits at the counter and places an order. Bruce speaking in deep and crisp voice says, "Hi I'll have steak medium rare with potatoes." He leans over and peers at Sam and Duke, he knows they're the ones that stopped him from feeding earlier, and he's not happy about it. He thinks about slapping them across the face but the place is crowded and he isn't ready to reveal his true self just yet. Soon his plate arrives he digs into the steak, which is red on the inside just like he likes it along with a side of potatoes. After finishing up, Bruce leaves his payment on the counter for the waiter and heads to the restroom, where he finds a new victim at the sink. He's never too full for a drink of blood, so he goes in for it grabs the man by the neck and instantly sticks his fangs into him till he drinks to his fill. Then he dumps the man into a stall, washes his hands, wipes his mouth and casually leaves out. Before leaving he takes a final look at Sam and Duke, smirks and leaves. Duke finishes his plate and thinks it was a good meal. He tells Sam he going to go the bathroom and drops some cash on the table. He walks right in goes up to the sink and washes hands. As he glances in the mirror he notices a man slumped over. Duke is alarmed and rushes to help the victim, who's lying motionless with blood running from his neck. He tries to wake him, he pats the man's cheek, but it doesn't work. Also he notices the bites on his neck and says, "Oh no, it's a vampire." He rushes out of the restroom to get Sam and help. Duke rushes over to the cashier and tells that someone was attacked in the bathroom, and orders him to call the police. Then he goes over to Sam and says, "Someone was attacked in the bathroom, I found him slumped over with a neck bite." Sam is surprised and says, "So he was here all along! And clearly not in bat form, maybe we can get a look at the surveillance camera to see what he looks like." Duke decides to go back over to the scared cashier and introduces himself "I am with the FBI and I would like to look at the surveillance camera while we wait for the police, maybe I can help ID the person before PD arrives." Duke's fake badge looks convincing enough to the cashier, so he goes over to get the manger to help. The manager walks up and takes Duke to the office allowing them access to the videos. He rewinds the tape and they both notice a tall man approaching the counter, and see he was the last person headed towards the restroom. That's proof enough for Duke who says, "Got him, that's all I need for now. I got a look at him. Now we've got to figure out which way he went." They ponder over the possibility that the vampire was tracking them and took someone else out instead of them. They thank the manager and leave the restaurant office. When they get back in the dining area they notice the police are there, and walk right out of the diner. Duke says "Let's go searching in the woods." They get in the car and head out after the vampire out in the outskirts of the town, hoping to find a clue. Duke says "Going into the layer is going to be tough because we don't know what to expect and he already has our scents, so we won't be able to sneak in." Sam agrees, "Fine, we can rush in full force if we find the hideout."

Finally Sam and Duke are deep in the woods, it's very calm and quiet. As they continue on they soon find a place that catches there attention. They hang back away from the cabin in question watching with binoculars. They notice the front of the cabin has a few cars out front, it appears to be large and normal looking from the outside.

Except they notice a broken window on the top floor that's completely covered with a cloth. Sam says, "Hey let's go check it out up close." They've got to get a peek in through one of the windows to be sure what's going on and if it's the right place. "No wait a minute," says Duke as another car arrives in front, two men get out, and they open the trunk and pull out containers filled with dark read liquid, blood! They enter into the house and greet the others. Duke thinks they definitely have the right place "Normal people don't bring containers of blood home!" It looks like they are about four or five vampires inside but they can't see the vampire from the woods. "Looks like we've found their layer, do you think we should go in now?" asks Sam. Duke says, "No, let's get more supplies and comeback. There could be more inside plus captives." Sam agrees. They quietly return to the car, start the engine, and pull off. Duke says, "It's disgusting, you know no matter how many vampires we come across there always seems to be more. We should torch the entire place before they grow and take over the city." They continue to drive quickly through the woods and arrive back in town to get their supplies and arsenals.

It's now nightfall and back at the cabin the vampires are talking and arranging coffins around away from the center of the room. There are a few victims chained inside, they're all too weak to let out screams. No one would hear them even if they could because no one is around, no nosey neighbors peering through their windows to see "what's going on." Bruce explains that if they blacken out all the windows it will look suspicious, so he wants all of the coffins moved down stairs. The others listen and begin carrying the coffins downstairs, one at a time. Down stairs is dark and cold, a perfect, and peaceful nesting place for vampires. They proceed to paint the windows black. Bruce says, "I like it better this way, I don't want to be a yuppie vampire sleeping in a bed, this is the way to roll, he laughs." So does his mates. One of the other vampires wants to know if they'll go into to town to feast. Bruce states, "We've got a problem, while in the woods I was interrupted by pesky vampire hunters, and we can be sure they're coming to look for us." But he's not worried and plans to stay and shouts "Lets feast on their blood when the time comes!" Another vampire excitedly agrees but they realize hunters can bring real trouble. As sometimes there are only one or two but they slaughter everyone in sight. So having hunters in town could certainly ruin their plan of expansion. Bruce says "When we're large enough we can take over the entire town and wipe the floor with those two." He laughs, as he adjusts the collar of his jacket. Bruce and the other vampires head out into their car ready for destruction. It's a dark night, the air is crisp and a bit foggy. The streets are busy with people going from here and there. Which makes the vampires very excited, as they could pick anyone to bite like hanging fruit. "We're going for a little entertainment tonight guys, I feel in the mood for a little action," says Bruce. Tonight he is determined and completely fearless. Soon they head over to a busy club that's seems to be very popular with the locals. They enter in with ease as they're sharply dressed and look impressive. The noise is loud and it's crowded inside but that won't stop Bruce, not tonight. For this is the start of his master plan. Two of his men grab the bouncers and snap their necks easily as if they were twigs, shut the doors and let the games begin. They grab person after person, biting and tearing them apart. Its total chaos, people are screaming and trying to get out but it's too late the doors are jammed shut! Tables are turned over, seats are thrown about and no one can hear their screams from the outside. These vamps are out for a buffet! They completely annihilate everyone inside, then head out completely satisfied. Bruce says, "Tonight is just the beginning, we're going to unleash havoc like no one has ever seen. Tonight was beautiful, well done. How about one more, are you guys up for it?" The others cheer in agreement, they're ready! They head for the next club and do the same thing, bodies are laid all over the floor, and it's been an hour of endless slaughter. Soon they finish up and head back to their layer, feeling completely happy with themselves.

They're sure that they've taken out one hundred or more people in one night. Meanwhile Sam and Duke have finished shopping and have found a hotel for the night. The hotel's pretty nice, it has large windows with a view, and they've done far better than their usual motel. The place looks good. Sam wonders how Duke scored such a great place. He says, "The town has very few hotels so the price was good and my card worked." Sam's happy to finally rest in a posh place, they're ready to go hunt vampires, and it's what keeps them busy from real life issues. "So we're stocked up on supplies. Think we should go back tonight for the vampires?" Sam agrees and says, "I think we've got everything we need, but we've got to go back to the hospital to check on James.

However, there's a knock on the door. Duke approaches the door slowly and peers through the peep hole. He sees a tall slender man in a uniform with an anxious look on his face. Duke opens the door slowly with his gun by his side. He's greeted by a hotel clerk, who informs them that staff is going room to room to tell guest about the city imposed curfew. Because the police say there are homicidal maniacs on the loose. Duke asks what happened. The clerk tells them he heard over the radio that two nightclubs were attacked and everyone was slaughtered, using his finger to slit his throat for emphasis. He tells them to check the news for more. Duke is surprised and tells the hotel clerk they'll stay in and check the news for more details. He thanks the hotel attendant and shuts the door behind him. Then looks over towards Sam and says, I think this is our vampire." Sam says, "I think so, but there may be more of them than we thought." They turn on the TV and hear the story of slaughter at the clubs, the body counts are high. Even Duke is stunned by the gruesome details and video footage in the quaint town.   Sam says, "We need to get over there and get a better picture of what we're dealing with." They counted about five vampires at the cabin earlier but the carnage looks like the work of a whole lot more. Duke agrees stating they may need some back up. Sam has a bright idea and says, "Hey, you know who's not far away from here?" Duke faces Sam and says, "No don't say it!" Sam says, "No, Isaac could be of some help he's smart and would fit in here perfectly, I'll call him." Sam whips out his shiny blue Smartphone and dials him.

3

Awakening

When he gets off the phone he tells Duke that Isaac has agreed to help and will be there soon. They decide to go over some gear and discuss whether they should risk breaking the curfew. Duke says, "The police force is unlikely to catch these guys anyway, if we go as the Feds we can get up and close to the scene." Sam agrees as they get dressed and talk about the carnage shots on the news.

Back at the hospital James is lying in bed stirring in his sleep. His dreams are erratic with images of being hungry in the woods with blood dripping from his mouth, and he's practically sweating up a storm. It's as if the bite marks are running deeper into his neck and increasing his hunger. He doesn't know what is before him. James is restless and as his hunger grows his fangs start to appear. He quickly awakes with a jolt completely hungry, and gets up from his bed feeling stronger and starving for something to eat. He glances at his meal tray, he tries a bit but doesn't feel anything, it isn't filling his taste buds. So he walks out of the room, realizing exactly what he needs! He quietly walks over to the next room, finds a patient sleeping peacefully till James reaches over and bites him, and proceeds to suck his blood. However, a nurse opens the door, she's surprised at the grotesque sight, as thoughts of confusion and disgust runs through her mind. She screams and blurts out, "What are you doing?" James slowly turns with blood dripping from his mouth, looks directly at the nurse and growls. He contemplates moving on to her for his next meal, but before he has a chance the frightened nurse runs off to the nurse's station to get some help. While still feeling quite hungry, James decides to run through the hospital attacking other patients to fill his hunger. There are screams and chaos throughout the hospital, while the staff try to contain things. Yet they are not prepared for such an event. Soon they manage to find James, who is cornered in a room and ready to attack like a fierce wild beast. Security comes in as back up for the doctor and nurses, as they rush and grab a hold of him. Then a doctor quickly inject James with something that puts his lights out like a sweet baby. They proceed to get him back in bed and strap him down completely, as they don't need or want a repeat of what just happened. They don't know what to think of his case, so they ponder that it could be cannibalism or rabies. Doctor Hudson is the lead doctor on staff for the night and orders to keep him sedated till he can have a psychological evaluation done. She then orders the nurses to carefully tend to the bite victims.

Meanwhile, back at the hotel, Sam says, "We already know the vampire's layer location, we just need to figure out the best time to attack them when they're the most vulnerable. Daytime?" Duke says, "No, sunrise when they go in for rest is probably the best time. But in the meantime let's go to the scene to check it out. Then we need to get over to the hospital to check on James. See if he has any signs of changing," as he grabs his coat. They head out to the crime scene at the club. The streets are clear but a crowd has formed near the entrance.

They can hear people talking as their faces express their shock and fear. Duke parks the car to the side, then he and Sam grab their FBI badges. They flash them at the cops in the entrance and when they arrive inside they see the carnage everywhere. The walls are splattered with blood, some body parts are scattered about, but they keep their composure. Because they're pros and have seen whole lot worst in all their years of hunting. Duke gets a long stare in his eyes and says to Sam that maybe the Vampires have taken a few people back to the cabin. He adds this could turn out to be a whole lot of trouble if those start to turn and are let lose. Sam says, "I know but there's no way we can get them all!" Duke disagrees and says, "I bet we can! It may be tough but we're not running from a fight." He pats Sam on the back for a little encouragement and suggest they clear out and head over to the hospital, because James could be a real dangerous situation if he turns. Sam walks over to the lead officer on the scene and says, "There doesn't appear to be any survivors but my partner and I will check with the locals to see if they can identify anyone, please keep us updated." He hands over a crisp white business card and they walk out, as the officer nods and waves them out.

They get back into the car and decide to go directly over the hospital. Sam says, "What do you want to do with James, take him out of the hospital and kill him somewhere else?" Duke replies, "No, easy there! If he hasn't had any blood I think we can give him the kit and drop him off with a family member to give it to him. Otherwise he'll turn and kill more innocent people to fill his hunger and then we'll have to kill him." Once at the hospital, it's

22

seems pretty quiet and everything appears to be back in order. When Duke walks over to the nurse's station he learns from the staff that the first victim went haywire and attacked patients. They discuss how James even tried to attack staff and was later subdued by a doctor. James is back in his room and heavily sedated as they walk into the room. They check the chart and scan the remarks. Looking at James lying helpless in bed makes them feel sorry for him. Sam looks at Duke says, "Everything's happening so quickly and James is really just a victim but now we face a major dilemma. How to kill a vampire inside of a hospital without bringing any attention to ourselves." Before Duke can answer a doctor walks in and greets them. She says that he will awake soon, if he's calm and back to normal he should be released tomorrow afternoon after a psych evaluation. Doctor Hudson adds, "James isn't suffering from any physical injuries and was there for observation and the bite wound, which has seemed to heal really quickly." Sam says, "I see and adds as long as there are no more outburst we're going to finish up the case as well." Also Duke states that they are still following leads on the attacker. Doctor Hudson nods and says that she hopes that they find the attacker soon. She heard there was an attack on a club not far from there. She says, "Perhaps we will know more about James's attack after the psychological evaluation." She closes the file and places it back in the file slot on the door and says goodbye to the agents.

Sam and Duke also leave the room and walk off to the side in the hallway to discuss their next move. Duke says "We can't kill him here" and Sam agrees. He says, "Definitely not, but we can catch

23

up with him when he's released and take care of it then. Otherwise he's going to attack again." Duke suggest they get a couple of kits for the two patients who were attacked. But first they turn back to go inside and find James gone. Now they feel some urgency and rush over to other rooms of the other two bite victims and they're gone as well! Duke is surprised and can't believe they got away, and wonders where in the world are they? Sam hopes they aren't bat vampires as well, because that will make their hunt a whole lot harder. Now they must assume that the bite victims are vampires and going to attack someone, so the kits are off the table. "We've got to hurry, because this town is about to have a real fight on their hands," Duke exclaims. Sam says, "Yeah let's go."   He mentions if they join the other vampires it could be really bad news for the town. Next, they head out of the hospital, and start to drive around the area hoping the new vampires have not gotten very far. Duke keeps a look out for them, he says, "I am sure they're still wearing their hospital gowns, so they should be easy to spot." Sam laughs and shouts, "Hey I think I saw something, make a turn there." They follow down a small street and see one of the two hospital victims walking. They stop the car, get out and slowly approach him. The fanged vampire growls at them and lunges right for them. A fight starts, Sam stabs him directly in the heart, stopping him in his tracks. They keep going and try to keep up the momentum, as they still have James and one more patient lurking the streets out for blood.

Sam says, "Alright let's go, maybe we can get to other one before he feeds." Duke agrees. They get back into the car and find patient number two heading into a grocery store. They see him preying on the store clerk, who fearfully tries to throw something at him. However, the vampire is relentless and continues to move forward, jumps over the counter and pushes the clerk down. The impact from the fall is hard but the clerk tries to fight back. The vampire's fangs are sharp and pointy and he wants his first meal. Yet, before he has a chance to stick his fangs into the store clerk Sam and Duke enter just in time. They grab him off the store clerk and drag him outside. Duke holds him down tightly, and can clearly see that the man is gone and nothing lies behind his cold dark eyes but a bloodthirsty vampire. They tell the clerk they're FBI agents and will take care of him. They exit the store drag the vampire away from the store and kill him in the alley. Afterwards they continue their search, but James is nowhere in sight! They've been searching for a while and it looks like James has gotten away. Sam says, "Because James has already fed we need to get him before he turns more people. " Duke agrees and says, James's long gone now and he wished they could have cured him, as he hit's the steering wheel out of frustration. After driving around for what feels like hours, they decide to go back to the hotel to get some rest and drive to layer in the morning with Isaac. They've been out the entire day, so they need to rest and refuel for the next day.

Meanwhile, Bruce and his minions continue to wreak complete havoc over the local pool halls and other nightspots. Unfortunately, the police are unable to catch them or put out the fire of negative reports via television. Yet after a long night the sun's approaching. Bruce with blood dripping from his mouth decides they've done enough for one night, so they head back to their layer. Deep in the woods some of the other vampires are hanging out in front of the cabin and enjoying the night. Now we learn that they are at least 10 males there. Bruce approaches them and high fives them. He says, "This has been a successful night, keep it up and the city will be ours. I've got two members to welcome into our family. Help them out of the car and tie them up inside." The guys are pleased with themselves, walk over to the car and take out two young men. They discuss the plan for a takeover and agree it will work out perfectly. They feel as if very soon they will have their own town. A vampire town for vampires and run by them. To show off their strength and importance in the world. It will be free from hunters and normal folks, with the exception of human livestock. Bruce says, "Tomorrow we'll take down the police station and add some officers to our family, we're going to need them on our side and once we have jobs in the station everything will start to appear legit." The others agree tomorrow will be a day of success.

  Meanwhile Duke and Sam arrive at the hotel. Sam checks his phone, and he gets a message from Isaac saying he'll be there by morning along with a friend. Duke goes to lay down and says, "We could use the help but things could get out of hand, like how will we control Isaac if he changes, I don't know who's stronger a vampire or a werewolf." Sam agrees with a smirk. They discuss the destruction the vampires have let out on the town. It has been a complete surprise, as most of vampires they've encountered try to live below the radar. But if their numbers grow, they're going to need a whole lot of hunters to fix the problem. It's getting late, Sam turns off the lights to gets some much needed sleep. At sun rise, the town is quiet and still in shock. But none of it has affected the birds, whom are chirping as usual. The light shines through the window as the brothers' rise. Duke and Sam feel refreshed after a good night's sleep. Duke goes to the window and let's in some sweet fresh air from the mountain top, and takes in the view of the town. They booked a nice room this time and they can see most of the town from their room. Sam rushes for the shower as Duke reminds him not to use up all the hot water, Sam laughs and says, "He'll do his best." As Duke waits he calls Isaac to see if he's nearby, because they'll definitely need him tonight. Sam's now back and checks with Duke, who tells him that Isaac is about 10 minutes away. Sam says, "Good we'll meet him at the town's entrance and fill him in on the details."

Back at the cabin the Vampires are all awake and heading for the local police station. They want complete control of the town! They pile into their black SUV. Bruce is at the wheel as he and his cronies head into the station. It's peaceful out with a few people trying to walk their dogs as if nothing has happened. They feel this is the perfect place for them. When they finally get to the station it's pretty quiet as everyone's busy trying to solve last night's murder. Two men block the door so that no one can enter the station and no one but them will leave out of it. Bruce is sure of himself and walks straight up to the front desk and addresses the officer. He politely inquires, "Who's in charge here?" The deputy is a medium height man who doesn't want to be disturbed, but says the sheriff's in charge and

27

busy. He asks, "How can I help you?" However Bruce is in no mood for quaint pleasantries, and without an answer he grabs the deputy and tosses him to the wall. This happens all too quickly before the deputy has a chance to draw his gun. He hit's the wall and is out cold and unresponsive. The commotion immediately brings the attention of the other officers, who shout at Bruce to stand still and put his hands up! Yet it's of no use, as the rest of the men start to attack the officers. Gun shots are fired, gun smoke fills the room, but the Police immediately notice that the bullets are having no effect. They begin to wonder what kind of people they are dealing with. The station gets very bloody as the fighting is back and forth. The Police try to keep the vampires at bay, but the vampires start feasting on some of the other officers. In the midst of the commotion another officer in the back places a call for help over the radio, but it's too late! Bruce tells the others they will keep the Sheriff and five men. He then orders five of his men to remain behind to clean the place up. He tells them to get uniforms, put them on and take control of their station. Now any emergency calls will go straight to them and keep work quiet. Two vampires take the hostages to the car and head back to the cabin in the woods. Bruce remains behind. Soon the station is cleared of the dead and completely clean. They decide to keep anyone who's breathing to bleed out completely.

After a while everything's in order and the vampires are in police uniform, Bruce takes on the role as sheriff, he looks the part and begins deleting files and photos. He requests a press conference for a special announcement! When the camera men and team arrive Bruce begins, "The Sheriff has fallen ill, so I'll be the new Sheriff of Placerville." He adds, "I want the people to know that we're working hard and have caught two of the attackers, but some are still at large so be careful while carrying on with your daily routines." He then officially removes the curfew, which will make everyone much happier as it's the weekend and everyone's looking to relax and have fun. While sitting at the town's entrance Sam and Duke hear the report from the station, and immediately wonder what's going on as they couldn't have the vampires. But whatever it's it will have to wait. As they talk, Isaac and his friend arrive at the town's entry. Duke and Sam get out the car to greet him, and they're happy he came and brought some help. They greet one another, Sam asks how they are doing. Isaac is doing well and is his usual chipper self. He introduced his friend Paul, who is tall, fit and looks strong enough to take on the vampires they'll surely have to fist fight. Isaac explains that they are glad to help and are sorry that he couldn't rustle up more help. But it's hard to convince a pack of werewolves to travel out to fight vampires. They'd rather just keep to their own territory. Duke nods, and starts to give a rundown of what happened so far, and informs them that they're looking at about ten or more vicious vampires. He explains how they tore through the town last night, leaving a huge body count. Sam explains that they originally thought there was only one vampire bat, but now it looks like he came to town with others. He tells them about the vampire cabin far out in the dark woods. He believes that they're here to stay, and are ready to kill anyone and everyone in their path.

4

On The Loose

Duke's already pumped to go after it, he hates
vampires and is sick of them popping up all over the
place. He wants to get started right away, and take
out as many as we can before sunset! Isaac and Paul
are on board. Werewolves and vampires don't get
along. Because vampires have an unrelenting greed,
while werewolves can manage their hunger far
better.

      However, before they head to the cabin, they
remember the police station report and choose to go
there first. As the whole story seems fishy and
they'd like to be sure everything is fine. So Isaac
parks his car along the side of the road behind a big
tall tree, then he and Paul jump into Duke's car.
They all head to town and arrive at the station. First
they drive around it to make sure no one's is
hanging out back, the coast looks clear. They're
cautious and don't want to walk right into a trap.
They see no signs of vampires, so they all get out of
the car, grab their badges and head in to the police
station to see what's going on. Sam and Duke walk
up to the front desk, they're dressed well in blue
suits, hair slicked back, looking very professional.
Duke goes first, he loves playing detective, and he
removes his sunglasses, flashes his FBI badge and
ask about the two men the officers captured. The
front officer sharply explains they have everything
under control and reiterates that the new sheriff has
a wining plan. Duke's not really convinced so he

says, "That's great but where are the guys you captured?" The officer explains that they were killed when they tried to flee, so their cases are officially closed. Sam questions if they can we see the bodies. But the front officer says no and explains it's their jurisdiction and would rather not have them involved. Before Sam and Duke can speak, the officer stands up, and says, "I am sorry but I've got to head to the back, for any more information you'll have to make an appointment." They notice everyone around seems a bit suspicious, but decide to go as they've been stonewalled. They say goodbye adding that they'll check in with Sheriff later in the day. As they walk out Sam asks, "Is it just me or are those guys acting a bit strange?   And who's the new sheriff and his "wining plan?" Duke agrees and says it's clear that something went down, but they will have to see to it later because they want to get to the vampires cabin before sunset.

Then they drive off for the cabin, intent on making the vampires pay! While driving in the car, they discuss the cops' behavior earlier and agree that something's off with the story. Duke talks about the weird front desk officer and how he seemed to come with a prepared answer really quickly. He says that it's likely they killed a couple of vampires, but they probably left the morgue at sunset completely unnoticed. However, the police station issue will have to wait. Sam spots the cabin and motions over in its direction. They notice that a couple of windows have been blackened out to keep the sun out. No one appears to be walking around in front today. They park, head out of the car and are fearlessly ready to exterminate vampires. Because

31

they've seen the vampire's ruthless killings at the clubs, they want to dish out some payback. The cabin looks peaceful on the outside but they know what lurks inside. They grab their large machete knives, a couple of shot guns and some dead man's blood, just in case. Then they go around the back of the cabin. Sam sticks a small knife in the lock with metal pick and smoothly pops the lock and quietly enter the place. The cabin is dark even though it's still day out and quiet enough to hear a pin drop. It's just the perfect place for vampires. Isaac and Paul head upstairs while Duke and Sam go downstairs. They walk slowly creep to sides and the corners of the hall. Suddenly over to the far right Sam notices a sleeping area, in it appear to be about five sleeping vampires lying down in open black coffins with satin interiors. They slowly approach the warm dark room. Then Duke pulls out his machete, and completely cuts off the head of first one, before it opened its eyes or let out a scream. Sam follows suit and hurriedly starts slaying the others before the remaining vampires awake. They finish them off and walk to the next room. Inside he finds a few officers and the real sheriff lying down. Sam says, "I think I found the sheriff and a few officers, but they all have neck bites. I am not sure if they've started to feed." He questions if they should kill them. But Duke tells him to finish the rest and come back for them.

Afterwards they head downstairs to where Isaac and Paul are, but they find no one except a few empty coffins. Duke starts to discuss the officer's behavior at the police station and how strange they acted. He now suspects that they're vampires incognito. And their act was to stonewall them from investigating and finding out the truth. Sam agrees, and says, "Yeah they're trying to keep everything under wraps." Isaac says he also thought everyone seemed strange and he thought there was a faint smell of blood when they walked in, but he didn't see any. Paul agrees and adds there was a faint smell mixed with ammonia. They urgently decide to return to the station, as leaving them could pose more danger for the town. They can't leave them till nightfall because they'll be out for blood. Duke frowns, grabs hold of the machete, clinches his teeth and says with a smirk, "We're out for blood to, and we're not taking any prisoners!" He then tells the guys to take the officers out of the cabin and says they're going to torch the whole damn place. Isaac and everyone agree and walk back upstairs to the sleeping officers and carry them out on to the front area. Isaac and Paul open the car trunk and look around for flammables but fine nothing. Yet Duke and Sam have found plenty of lighter fluid in the storage cabinet in the kitchen, so they begin pour it all over. Duke turns on the gas form the stove to ensure the cabin's demise. They calmly leave out feeling happy with themselves. Then Sam takes out a book of matches, strikes the box and watches the warm flame light, he then tosses the match through the front door. He's got a smile on his face as he watches everything catch fire. Within a few seconds a loud explosion goes off and they take the officers to the car. Sam suggests they use the kit on the officers and bring them to the hospital. He wonders if he can get the doctor they met earlier to continue giving it to them. Duke agrees and hopes to find the other vampires to get the town back to normal. Unfortunately, two of the

officers look pale and are barely alert. Sam takes
their pulse and says he can't find one. Duke decides
it's best to leave them in front of the cabin and call
in a 911 call, they cover them and leave them for
the ambulance. They drive off with only the sheriff
who's still breathing normally.

Meanwhile at the police station the
remaining pack of vampires are looking for their
next target. They want the town and nothing's going
to get in their way. Bruce mentions it would be a
good idea to hit the remaining nightspots and some
homes. He says, "The town is ripe for the picking."
But it's getting late and Bruce decides to go back to
the cabin leaving a few men in charge of the station.
Upon arrival the vampires see the complete
destruction of their home and become angry. Bruce
is visibly upset and shouts out and tosses heavy
rubble across the front in anger. They begin to look
through the damage, the cabin is still standing but
completely burned out. Bruce says he picks up the
scent of the same men from the forest along with
some others. He tells the others that the hunters
have gone too far! Bruce says, "They need to be
stopped and I vow to turn at least 10 men into
vampires tonight, to make up for our lost." He then
orders two of his men to follow the human scents
that they've picked up. While he finds another place
further down to secure before sunset. "This town
will be ours!" exclaims Bruce.

Soon Duke and Sam arrive at the hospital
with the sheriff. He's too weak to walk so they
carry him and tell him that he'll be fine and to hang
in there. The hospital staff immediately comes to
their aid with a stretcher. Doctor Hudson sees them
from the work station and walks over to them, says

34

hi and asks what happened? Sam explains that the sheriff is a bite victim like the other patients from yesterday. He tells her that they've got the only medicine that can help him. He explains this is a very serious situation and asks her if she can give him the medicine, while they hunt for the attackers. The doctor is hesitant at first, but agrees and assures them that she will have a nurse administer it promptly. They strap the sheriff down for his own good and assign a room for him where the nurse will be on watch. She asks Duke "How long does it take for the medicine to work?" He says a few hours and then he should start to feel normal again. Doctor Hudson nods in agreement and thanks them for their help. Then Sam and Duke say goodbye and head back to the car with Isaac and Paul waiting inside. Back in the woods the vampires hurriedly get to finding a new home out in the woods. Soon enough Bruce finds one and says, "This will have to do, it's getting late." They open the door, it's empty, cool and dark. The cabin looks like it will work wonderfully for them. Soon they begin getting ready for tonight's mission. Sam and the guys are sitting in the car heading to the town square, as they figure it's the best place to see what's happening in the town after sunset. It's starting to get dark, the town has a grey, cloudy haze around it, the weather's mild, and they sit and chat. The town's people are scarcely out, definitely afraid after the horrifying attacks of the previous night. A few people are here and there along with the usual empty stragglers going in and out of an all-night market. As they sit in the car they decide to turn on their cop radio to listen out for anything. They hear a home invasion call come in, the report says:

"Rabid men on the loose." Duke thinks this sounds like something they should check out. And says it looks the vampires have gone back to sneaking through windows. They rev up the engine, it's loud and vibrates. Sam says, "Maybe we can catch them this time." So the brothers drive over to call. Soon they arrive at the home and park out front. They notice the neighborhood's ambience. It's quiet with dimly lit street lights, very clean and definitely a place they'd be happy to call home. Duke reaches over Sam to go into the glove compartment to grab their badges. He tells Isaac and Paul to stay in the car and to keep a look out for anything suspicious, while they go talk to the family. Isaac says, "If you guys don't come back in 10, we'll come look for you." Duke and Sam walk up towards the house, noticing the vampire police are with the family conducting an interview. They see a middle aged man of fairly good shape and size sitting on the sofa describing what happened. They enter, flash their badges for the officer waiting by the door. He waves them inside and they decide to hang back and listen in. The father tells how two men came into his home and tried to attack him. He describes how he had to fight with one while the other ran away. He says, "I managed to get my gun and fired it, but it only slowed him down a little."   He then describes how suddenly the attacker tried to be bite him. The officer says, "I think it's one of the rabid men on the loose."   The father tells them he hit the attacker really hard, but he only ran off when his cat came blazing in screeching and hissing. His kids were home safely hiding in a locked closet, so the other burglar never saw them. Duke looks around and sees the kids sitting in the kitchen drinking

36

what looks like juice while an officer does his best
to keep them distracted. The officer takes down
everything in his pad and says he's glad that
everyone's safe, and he has officers looking for the
attackers. Also he reminds the victim to board the
broken window and lock the doors. The officer
stands up hands him a card to call if he remembers
anything else and tells him he'll be in touch. The
officer then turns to the remaining officers to inform
them that they have what they need and can leave.
He notices Duke and Sam, and simply waves on the
way out. But it's too late because Sam and Duke
know the police are really vampires and turn around
to meet them outside. Duke walks over and says,
"Hey vamp police are you done playing human,
we've got a bone to pick with you." The vampire
officer's growl, and their sharp fangs begin to show.
The lead officer arrogantly says, "We're ready for
you anytime, this town is ours and we're not
leaving." This angers Sam and he takes a swing at
one cop, and tells him you're not taking anything! A
fight ensues, the vampire police are put up a strong
fight and do their best to block the fierce blows that
Sam and Duke hand out. Suddenly Duke injects the
first officer with dead man's blood and then the
other, bringing them to a halt. The vampires drop
and instantly feel weak and confused as to what just
happened. It doesn't matter though because they're
too weak to fight. Sam and Duke grab the vampires
and put them in back of the police car. Then Duke
walks up to Isaac and Paul and says, "Hey we're
going to take them further down the road, keep an
eye on things and we'll meet you back here." Isaac
agrees as he notices the police car filled with
vampires in police uniforms. Duke and Sam drive

them to a deserted area and question the vampires there. They tie one against a tree and begin their questioning. Sam asks where's the leader and what did you do with the real police force? The vampire officer explains that they're all dead except only a few with them. He tells them to give up and go away because the town is theirs. Duke disagrees and shrewdly says, "Not going to happen, where is your leader?", as he boldly slaps him across the face. The vampire uses his shoulder to wipe the blood from his mouth, smiles and says, "Oh its happening and you'll never find him, he'll find you first!" Duke's temper has started to kick in at this point, so he says; "I've had it with this one." He slaps him one more time to reiterate his feelings. However the vampire growls back and tells him they will never reveal the truth to them. He says, "We've got the numbers and we will take this town!" Sam looks at Duke and says, "Yeah that's enough" and cuts the vampire's head off. It drops to the ground with a thump, now the problem just got smaller. They untie what's left of the vampire and lay it on the ground. Duke supposes they'll have to dig a grave somewhere in the back.

Next Sam grabs the second vampire who's witnessed the fate of his comrade. He tells him to talk if he wants to save his life as he leans in closer to intimidate him. They start in on him asking him multiple questions, though it's of no use as he won't talk. And now they are no closer to finding the leader and it's starting to get late enough for more vampires to begin roaming the streets. Duke makes a fast decision to kill the last one so they can start looking for the rest of the vampires. They begin digging a grave in the wooded area to place the bodies inside. But before they do Sam drives a knife straight into each one's heart to be sure. Then they fill the hole with dirt and decide to return back to the last house and search the area for more vampires. They decide to leave the police car at the location and wipe everything down ensuring not to leave any fingerprints behind, and abandon it. While walking back towards the car, they encounter two men wondering around in the back of an unsuspecting home. Both Duke and Sam think they've got another pair of vampires, so they walk up to them as Sam shouts out "Stop right there blood fiends!" The vampires see them, recognize them, draw their fangs, and ready themselves for a fight. They're tall and fit but the brothers are ready to battle and begin exchanging punches. Sam feels their strength but keeps fighting till the end. It pays off because soon Sam pins one vampire and kills him, while Duke fights the other one and makes work of him. Now both are dead, leaving them hopeful that they've decreased the vampire pact substantially. Now Sam has a chance to catch his breath, and says, "Whew, those guys didn't want to give up, and I think they knew us right away, sort of like they knew our scent." Duke agrees adding, "They probably picked it up from the cabin." They keep looking around for more vampires but nothing turns up, so they decide that the rest of neighborhood seems fine. And start walking back towards the car. Unfortunately, they are met by four more ghoulish looking vampires, clearly waiting to start something. Meanwhile back in the car Isaac starts to notice that a lot of time has passed and wants to go after Sam and Duke. Paul agrees and they leave the car taking along with a few knives just in case. As they begin walking around they hear some commotion and head that way.

5

Suspect Officers

One vampire with a small smirk on his face says: "Hunter's blood! This is going to be a pleasure. Maybe we can bring one back to Bruce." They walk up to them and a brawl starts. There's no time for questions. The second vampire a lot shorter that the first two says, "We knew it was you two that destroyed our layer, now you're going to pay!"

Soon Isaac and Paul meet up with them and manage to get the upper hand on the vampires, and the fighting comes to an end. The ghoulish vampires meet their end by grotesque decapitation! Sam wonders aloud just how many are there, realizing now the vampires may be searching for them. Even though Duke doesn't have an exact number, he feels they're ready and very motivated to get Placerville back to normal. Their numbers could be large and spread out, so Duke and the gang try to figure out where their next hit will likely be. Isaac reminds them about the vampires attacking the local police station during the day and wonder if they'd attack another open place. They consider it and decide to head back over to the station and deal with that situation. Sam adds, "Maybe the hit on the police station was for eliminating response to emergencies so that they can attack people at will." Duke agrees and thinks they need to ready themselves for a huge fight and reminds everyone to cover their necks to prevent being bitten easily.

They grab some cloth off the dead vampires and wrap their neck well.

Making sure to triple fold it for better protection. Next, they do their best to get rid of the corpses in the back area, to avoid leaving a trail of dead bodies all in one area. Then they walk back to the car, pile back in and head to the police station. Finally they arrive at the police station, Duke turns to everyone and ensures they are ready, they all agree in unison. Then they quietly leave the car and gather enough weapons to give the vampire police a good fight. They walk in guns blazing absolutely ready for a vampire battle. However there are fifteen vampires inside the station, likely more than their last visit. Sam walks up to the front desk and says, "The jigs up, we know that you're not real officers and asks where are the real cops?" The vampire officer looks Sam right in the eyes with conviction and says "They're all dead and you're going to join them!" as he flashes his fangs, leaps over the desk and starts to attack. Sam responds back with swift punches. The vampire police give a good fight and they are equally pumped to get a piece of the brothers, since their reputation is well known. Yet, Sam, Duke, Isaac and Paul do a brilliant job at defeating them, and the station becomes completely vampire free! Afterwards Duke tells Isaac to check the security cameras then erase any traces of them, while they quickly clean up the station. This is a piece of cake for Isaac because he's good at computer hacking. He takes charge of the task and goes off to the back office hoping to get into system and he does, since the chief has left his computer on screensaver instead of logging out. He finds the security footage and goes to work. Meanwhile San turns on the station radio to listen out for any more attacks. Isaac walks out of the office and announces that he took care of the security camera. And has left the vampire's attack on the real officers, so others can piece together a story. They hear over the emergency radio the local bowling alley requesting emergency response for a few violent killers on the loose. They believe it's another vampire case and decide to head over there. On the way out Duke thanks Isaac for taking care if the cameras and thinks his touches were a great idea. They hop in the car and head over to the bowling alley.

When they arrive on the scene they see people all around them screaming and running out of the bowling alley. The large trophy case is broken and despite the urgency of the scene, they see a few people looting. There is glass everywhere and the concession stand has been completely trashed. Clearly something terrifying is going on inside, so they grab arsenals before going inside. As Duke approaches the entrance he can see what appears to be vampires in the distance ripping into an innocent victim. Sam also notices, rushes over and fights with the vampires. He wraps his hand around the neck of one and with his other hand uses his sliver blade to stab the vampire in the heart. Duke, Isaac and Paul join in on the remaining vampires as everyone continues to run out. They keep fighting until they finish off the group, but Duke spots another vampire. Unfortunately they're too late as the vampire spots them and runs to save his life. Duke and Sam run after the vampire but lose him, because the crowd's still running in a panic. Soon the police from the next town arrive on the scene, and are completely shocked by everything. They do their best to calm everyone. The sound of blazing sirens resonate with the crowd as the panic starts to die down. The police call for paramedics and back up at the alley. Because these are real cops Sam and Duke decide it's time to get of there. Sam thinks it's a good idea, since there's nothing left for them to do at the alley.

Sam over hears another officer on his radio asking for help at the local shopping center because it's under attack by what's described as cannibal serial killers. It appears as if the vampires are ripping poor Placerville to shreds and may get the upper hand if not caught. The brothers finish up at the bowling alley, pile back into car to head directly over to the shopping center. Once they arrive at the center, it's apparent that they're too late. Fire trucks, ambulances and police cars are everywhere. People are tearfully leaving the mall, while some are in a panic screaming out of sheer fear. It's clear the shoppers are completely confused about what they've experienced. Sam and Duke proceed further in and flash their badges for full access. They're surprised to see many bodies lying about covered with sheets. They know this must have been a nightmare, and discuss the vampires growing numbers and bolder tactics. There's nothing that they can do at the mall, no one to punch in the face. Duke's upset and says, "We're too late!" as he hit's the wall in frustration. Isaac walks up and reminds them not to lose hope, and that they can save the town. He suggest they go back to the vampire's layer and look for clues on their next hit. They agree and leave the mall to head back to the woods. Meanwhile, Bruce and his vampires take five victims with them to their layer, to turn them into new vampires. He says, "Tonight was good and the towns people are ripe for the picking, let's feed and go door to door before sunrise." As he takes a victim and sinks his sharp fangs into his neck, while everyone watches the blood run from the screaming victim's throat. The other vampires join in and feed off their victims one more time.

Then Bruce speaks up to tell the others to put the newbie vampires indoors and wait for the hunger to grow inside of them. Once that starts to happen they will let them loose on the town for their first feeding. The vampires follow his orders, and walk the weak victims into the cabin. And put them in a dimly lit room along with a few water bottles. Downstairs Bruce thinks it would be a great time to go for another round of attacks in town. He's full of energy and hasn't felt this good in a hundred years. His men are receptive, but one of the vampires are worried and wonders out loud if there could be more hunters coming. Bruce says, "You're right, but if we continue to slaughter more lazy townsfolk, while turning others along the way, we'll have a large enough number to take them on and eliminate them once and for all." At that moment one of his men approaches him and whispers in his ears, "The hunters have been spotted nearby." "Good let them come here, let's us have our revenge for the destruction of our home and family. Let them come so that we my slowly feast on their blood and bleed them dry, and lye their filthy bones out back for the dogs." says Bruce. Meanwhile back in the car, Duke decides to head near the first layer, hoping they can find a clue on the new layer's whereabouts. Duke turns on the engine, revs it a bit and starts driving along the backwoods. Along the way Sam notices some activity near what looks like an abandoned place. He says, "Pull over to the side that looks like the right spot." It's dark out but they can hear the desperate shrieks creeping out into the woods. Duke pulls over, and kills the lights quickly and quietly get out. Then opens the trunk to pull out a few large knives and a 45 magnum filled with silver bullets. Everyone gets out and heads to the cabin, they slowly creep up to the cabin. But they encounter four aggressive large black dogs. They fire at them and decide to go in guns blazing. Which surprises and interrupts the vampires feeding. Duke and the others start heavily fighting. Yet the vampires are mad about losing their comrades and fight as hard as they can. Blood splatters all about as Duke and Sam decimate as many vampires as possible.

Unfortunately, the night gets harder, as a full moon creeps from behind the clouds. Both Isaac and Paul start showing signs of changing, though they try hard to fight it, but they feel it coming on. To catch their composer Isaac and Paul back out of the layer and go out for air, but it doesn't stop it from happening. Duke and Sam continue fighting as they see Isaac and Paul go out front. Duke goes after them and says, "Hey are you alright?" Isaac is struggling to hold it in, and lets out a deep growl, "No, I am changing right now." His eyes are yellow and hairs start popping out of his face and hands, as he burst through his clothes to display a fully wolfed out Isaac. Next to him Paul changes and he's a larger harrier wolf with sharp teeth and claws. Sam backs up and says, "Try to stay calm, see if you can control it, you guys are still inside there." But it's too late they've turned too quickly, they're hairy, ferocious with piercing yellow eyes that glow

45

in the dark. The werewolves then uncontrollably run into the cabin shocking Duke and Sam by their strength. They run into the cabin, ferociously fight against the vampires, screams are heard, blood gushes everywhere as a few try to run off. They are mortal enemies and wolves hate vampires.

Now the war becomes between werewolves and vampires. Soon it's obvious that the vampires are no match, and are ravaged. Sam thinks quickly and slams the doors shut to prevent Isaac and Paul from leaving, but they leap from a window and run out into the dark, cold forest. This is a big problem, and it leaves Duke and Sam wondering who will be the wolves' next victims. Duke's unhappy about this new roadblock and decides they need to go after them. However, Bruce appears ready to finish the job in full vampire bat form, his red piercing eyes glares harshly at them in rage! He approaches both Sam and Duke while outside, he's large and they've got their work cut out for them. They stand still and in awe of the size of the bat. He says, "I've heard all about you hunters, and we're sick of you coming here and interfering in our plans. We want this town, we deserve it, and the people are lazy and stupid. This town has potential, we will take it!" Duke says, "Not today!" as he charges towards Bruce, but is hit by Bruce's large wing. He falls and comes down pretty hard, for Bruce is a lot stronger than any vampire they've ever encountered. Sam wants to take him down, so he quickly fires a few shots at Bruce. But he's unfazed and arrogantly says, "Your pathetic bullets won't stop me you fools!" He's not going anywhere because he wants to ruin the town. Bruce tells them he wants the town for himself because the humans don't deserve it because they only care about their desires and smart gadgets.

Whereas the vampires will rule the town better and make families and form a true community. But first he walks closer to them and tells them in a sharp and evil tone that he will have his revenge, and he flies off like a bat fleeing a bright sunlit cave! Sam and Duke stare up in shock amazed by the size and speed of the vampire. Bruce goes off on his mission to let out his revengeful furry on the population and the wolves. He heads into the forest and swoops, between the trees high and low looking for the two werewolves. They are howling at moon, growling and full of anger. Bruce's eagle like vision sees them and he approaches swiftly. He grabs hold of Paul like a small toy and flings him, but Paul land's on his feet, then tries to take a crippling bite out of Bruce. However, it doesn't work and Bruce grabs him and takes him up for a flight and drops him to ground once again. Paul's motionless body lays on the forest floor. Next Isaac charges at Bruce and bites at his legs. Bruce growls and hits at the werewolf and they go back and forth till Isaac is slammed hard against the ground. Then suddenly Bruce averts his attention back to the town's people.

Meanwhile back at the cabin, Duke opens the door and checks out the layer, he looks around and takes in the scene. It's bloody inside, body parts lye thrown about, and there appears to be no survivors. They notice most of the vampires are dead many with their heads ripped off. It looks like both Isaac and Paul has caused much damage. Duke is surprised and says, "Wow I didn't expect this. But hey at least they got the job done." They slam the door shut and decide to go find Isaac and Paul in the woods, which will be hard because it's quite dark, even though there's some moonlight. Before getting into the car they reload their guns. Sam checks to make sure his older brother isn't hurt, he is bruised but okay. Duke tells him he's fine and that the fall didn't brake anything, but now he knows not to under estimate the vamp bat next time. He's going to shoot first, the hell with questions at this point.

The case has taken way too long and if they want to avoid a mass hysteria they've got to kill every single vampire, ASAP! Now Bruce is heading over to his next target, a local movie theater! He smoothly lands in the back of the theater and transforms back into man form. Two other vampires that managed to escape when the fighting started are waiting for him in the front. They see Bruce immediately and inquire regarding the hunters, he tells them it's not over but the two wolves are likely dead. He says, "I'll finish the other two later." They walk up to the ticket booth and politely purchase tickets to a new screening of a boring puke worthy, but surprisingly popular romantic comedy. They walk in and agree that this moment will be sheer enjoyment, as they walk in front the playing screen. One unsuspecting fool shouts out, "Hey sit down, we can't see!" Bruce smirks and glares his fangs, as he leaps into the crowd and starts ripping everyone to shreds. Chaos starts to ensue, people are running, screaming and trampling over one another, but the door is stuck! Only a few screaming people manage to squeeze through the gap to get away! Leaving Bruce and his pals to attack and drink blood to their fill.

Back in the woods Duke and Sam drive around but are unable to locate Isaac and Paul, because it's just too dark out. They turn on the radio to listen out for a wolf sighting, instead they hear a report of an attack at the local theater. Sam says, "It's the vampires again, it's got to be! " It's hard to believe but it definitely looks like this pack of vampires are relentless. They decide to head over to the call, hoping that they'll be able to save some of the people. Finally they arrive at the movie theater and park the car out front. There's a lot commotion out front, even the ambulances have arrived. Unbeknownst to them, they're too late to help because Bruce and his pals are already gone. Sam and Duke flash their badges and go in, it's another messy crime scene with no vampires or bats in sight. "He's not here, they got away, again!" exclaims Sam. Duke says, "I'll go the manager to find out what he knows. " They look around and deduce that Bruce must not have been alone. They ask the manager for the security tape. They view the whole bloody scene and see that Bruce was with two other vampires. Duke walks out of the office, thanks the manager and tells them to wait for the local police. He reassures him that they will start to look for the criminals. The shaking theater manager informs them that he's shutting the place down until further notice. Sam and Duke are upset but decide to keep looking and head back into the car in search for Bruce and the wolves. They discuss the events at the theater and Sam thinks they may need to call more hunters in to save Placerville. But Duke's hasn't lost hope yet and tells him that they can do it, all they need is the right opportunity.

6

The Fangs Come Out

However, Bruce and his pals are steps ahead of
them and have already started to enter a restaurant.
People are eating and enjoying themselves. Bruce
immediately goes in for the kill and the other
vampires start to attack patrons. Everyone starts to
panic, scream and run out of the restaurant. The
vampires turn over tables, toss food to the ground.
At this point they want to frighten everyone and
show them whose boss, so they repeat the carnage
of the movie theater. It's a bloody scene, some of
the staff manage to flee and save themselves.
However, most can't get out and are surrounded!
Sam spots something, and yells, "Stop the car!
What's going on over there?" Duke pulls over and
says, "Looks like we've found them. Let's go in."
They get out of the car and head straight for the
trunk to gear up. This time they've got a crossbow
ready with an arrow dipped in dead man's blood,
which is like poison for vampires. They enter the
restaurant fully ready to kick some vampire butt,
they look around and catch a glimpse of Bruce.
Who sees them first and shines a bloody smile at
them. Duke shouts out, "Hey Batboy!" As he aims
and shoots directly at Bruce, the arrow hits him in
the chest. He sneers and quickly orders his vampires
to split up, and turn four people and take them
along. They listen and quickly follows orders,
sneaking out the back. Sam fires another arrow and
rushes towards Bruce. The dead man's bloods gets
inside of Bruce, but it doesn't neutralize him right

away, so he rushes over towards Sam and Duke. "You've come back for more? Let's pick up where we left of," exclaims Bruce as he grabs a hold of Sam and slams him against the wall. Duke's upset and is quick to look out for his younger brother Sam by firing loads of dead man's blood bullets into Bruce. But he hasn't fallen yet so he walks up to Duke and starts to fight him.

Soon Sam manages to get up and pull himself together in time to join in. They both work on him and Bruce is bloody, yet very hard to take out. Bruce climbs on top of a table, rises and transforms into a bat. Then he jumps down and pushes Sam to the cold marble floors with his wing, and whacks Duke really hard with the other. Bruce turns towards Sam and slowly approaches him and says in a hauntingly deep voice, "Tonight I will feast on your blood and rid the world of one less hunter," while baring his long razor sharp fangs. He steps closer to Sam as he gallantly lunges towards him for a bite. Yet, Duke attacks him from behind, while Sam manages to get up. They fight intensely to bring Bruce down. Soon the dead man's blood begins to affect him, as his punches start to slow and he staggers a bit. Realizing something is not quite right, he rises up his sail like wings and shouts to them, "You think you're so smart don't you? I'll be back for the both of you, this is not over!" He jumps through the restaurant's front window, then takes off for safety leaving behind only shattered glass.

Soon Bruce arrives back at the cabin and the other vampires are waiting there with four new members. He tells them he's hurt and that the hunters have injected him with something. But he's happy to see that they've got more recruits. He orders them to keep them safe, and clean the place up. He says, "As we mourn for our dead brothers, we'll continue with our plan to take this town tomorrow." Another vampire asks about the hunters and wonders if they will come back to the cabin. Bruce says, "Yes, it's possible but I want you to find where they're living and pay them a visit, but be careful to avoid getting shot, as the hunter's arrows are laced with some sort of poisonous material, and is very nasty!" , while taking a seat. The vampire says, "Will do." Bruce wants them to give the new members some blood from the stock pile in the refrigerator. Then they'll rest during the day to be in their top form with full strength. Meanwhile Sam and Duke get into the car and drive around town looking for the other vampires until sunrise, but can't find them. The fog is approaching the town like a thick blanket and they're feeling extremely tired from vampire hunting. So they decide to head back to the hotel to get some much needed rest. Because they'll need it tomorrow if they want to capture Bruce. Soon they arrive at the hotel and take the elevator straight up to their room. Where the room is just as they left it, two big comfy beds just waiting for them. Sam goes to wash up, he lets the hot steam calm his aches and a few good lathers leaves him refreshed. Duke sits and waits, then decides to try Isaac's cell. But no one picks up. He notices Sam leaving the bathroom, "I tried Isaac and still no answer, we'll have to look for them first thing in the morning." "Sure thing, have a shower and get some rest," says Sam. Duke agrees and says, "Good night" as he heads for his shower. Afterwards, he comes out to find Sam fast asleep, and does the same, feeling happy that he and brother are safe and sound, for at least tonight anyway.

Next morning the sun's up and shines brightly through the rooms scenic windows. Sam enters the room with coffee and pie. They sit and talk, completely ready for whatever the day has to offer. They enjoy breakfast and surf the net for news on the town, but there were no unordinary 911 calls or stories. They figure the morning should be quiet considering how busy the vampire clan has been. Sam says, "When I was driving, I saw that Isaac's car is still where he left it. I think we should head back to the cabin maybe they're around there, plus we can search for the vampires." Duke replies, "Me too, but let's eat first. If we're going to stop them we need to pump way more dead man's blood into the leader." "Yeah it didn't stop him in his track but it's slowed him down. I am done, are you ready?" asks Sam "Yeah the pie was good, I feel good! Let's go," says Duke, while patting his stomach. They drive through the town, it's sunny and beautiful out. But trouble has left its mark on the town, some windows have been boarded, people are hurrying about, some are cleaning up the streets. Yet it's strangely peaceful out. They keep driving until Sam reaches the dark eerie cabin. He suggest they double the portions of their dead man's blood first, then go straight for the leader. Duke agrees, as they step out of the car and head to the trunk. They grab everything needed and quietly approach the cabin from the back. Duke easily picks the lock and they enter the place through the kitchen, it's quiet. So they decide to head upstairs where they find rooms on both sides of the hall. Sam opens the first door, and they find four new vampires sleeping upstairs. They're stirring a bit in their sleep, having already eaten in the middle of the night. Sam sees drops of blood on their mouths and shirts and concludes it's too late to save them. He whispers to Duke, "Hey, it looks like they've changed the victims from last night into vampires." Thus it's too late to save them, so they must kill them before they grow strong and attack more people, since vampirism spreads like a bad virus. Sam knows that he has no choice, so he pulls out his sharp knife, then swiftly and quietly drive it through the vampire's heart. They kill one at a time and finish the job by cutting off their heads ensuring that they won't come back for blood. Then they proceed to check the other rooms but there all empty. Sam says, "There's no sign of the leader, do you think he's gone somewhere else?" Duke is unsure and wants to stay close together as they cautiously proceed downstairs. They believe that the vampires are nesting, but could awake at any time.

The basement is very dark and all of the windows have been blacked out so that sunlight will not shine on a single thing inside. As Sam and Duke stroll deeper into the bottom level they see two coffins with the lids closed. Duke can feel his blood pumping faster, because they may have hit the jackpot with a grand chance to jab Bruce in his cold dark heart. However, it's terribly dark inside, so Duke decides to open a window to let in enough light to see well. Sam thinks it's better and asks, "Are you ready?" Duke tells him to wait as he gets something to tie the other casket shut, just in case the first one wakes. Sam nods in agreement and begins to look around for a bit and finds some rope to tie around the other coffin. Duke tells Sam to stand on the other side of the coffin before opening it. Duke stands with a sharp silver blade ready to stab whatever's inside. Sam takes a deep breath and gently opens the lid.   But it's not Bruce, it's another vampire, so Sam quickly stabs him before it has time to move. The vampire's yellow eyes open as a gush of blood bursts out of its mouth.

Then Duke moves in and uses his large knife to cut its head off, just to be sure it will not come back. He says, "There's one more to go." He walks over to the other coffin and begins to take off the rope so the he can open it. Duke really hope's its Bruce, so they can end this nightmare. They pause before opening it, Sam leans over the lid to listen for anything, but it's silent inside. He whispers, "Okay let's do this." He motions Duke to continue, then he opens the lid. With great surprise it's Bruce, who eyes immediately open and he jumps up quickly, as they move back. Bruce growls and says, "You two!" He then tosses Sam to the side and goes after Duke. He tells him, "This will be the last time that the two of you will interfere with my plans. I am going to break your arms and legs slowly, then I am going to turn your brother and when he comes around we will both drink every drop of your blood." Duke replies "How much you want to bet that you won't walk out this place alive?" He fires more dead man's blood into Bruce. Then walks right up to him and punches him in the face. Bruce hits back with heavy blows as he's determined to rid himself of the hunters. The coffins fall to the ground and light is coming in brightly. Even though the landing was hard on Sam, he slowly starts to come to and sees the fight. He reaches for his gun and lets out two bullets into Bruce, hitting him in the back. Then Duke hits more and stabs Bruce straight in the heart, kicks him down. Bruce tries fearlessly to fend him off, but he's got too much dead man's blood in him to function properly. They keep pounding him till he's pinned. Then Duke takes the final blow lopping Bruce's head completely off of his body.

Duke leans over Bruce's body and says, "You're not flying away this time batboy!" He then turns to check on his brother Sam. He's good and thankful to have had the chance to fire off a couple of shots into the vampire. He says with a small smile, "Five more like this guy and we're going to be at the top of our game." Duke now smirking replies, "Tell me about it, I don't want to know where he came from, but let's hope he's the last." They shove the vampires back into the coffins, carry them and the other dead vampire out to the backyard, dowse them with lighter fluid and set them to flames. They quietly sit and stare till the corpses are gone.

Afterwards Duke and Sam head out of the cabin, get back into the car and head out into the woods to look for their werewolf friends. Soon after much driving they finally see Isaac and Paul, who both look as if they've seen better days. Duke honks, stops the car and gets out to approach them. They greet them and wonder where have they been all night. "Nice duds", laughs Duke. Isaac says, "This is the best we could come up with man, considering our options." He explains after they bolted from the cabin they tried to wait out the change. They fed on the vampires so they weren't hungry, but they didn't want to risk moving around town. So they waited in the woods, but later into the night they heard a loud whooshing sound brushing through the trees. It happened quickly, and he says, "He saw a large bat zooming towards us." Paul agrees and tells them, "It grabbed me and took me high up in the sky and dropped me for death. At least that's what the vampire thought. Thankfully I landed on the bushes and only got knocked unconscious." He adds, "It didn't bite me, I feel a little bruised but at least I am still here." Isaac talks about how he fought with him a bit and describes its strength. But after sometime the vampire became distracted and bolted away, and then he took cover. He says, "It came at us pretty hard and we fought but of course being able to fly gave him an advantage. " Duke nods, and adds, "It was intense for us to, we were fighting him and it felt like we were getting close to killing him, but then all of sudden he took off and we couldn't catch him as well." Sam agrees and exclaims, "In the end we got every last one them, and even though at times I thought it was going to be impossible."

Duke tells them they did an awesome job inside the cabin. Afterwards, they went in to finish the job and cleared the place. They describe the numerous coffins that where filled with vampires and how they found several victims the vamps had turned, and how they had to be killed. He tells them, "The leader was by far the toughest to take down, and very unlike other vampires. It could fly and grew larger in size with almost no effort." Sam smirks and says, "He was full of himself, but in the end we took him down." Isaac and Paul think Duke and Sam did a great job as usual. They all stand and take in the nice scenery and fresh air. Isaac says, "Hopefully this town can get back to normal, it looks like a nice place to live." Paul agrees. The town was pretty welcoming. Even though they suffered vampire killers on the loose, many didn't completely freak out and lock themselves indoors till the coast was clear.

Duke thanks them again for their hard work and says, "We're grateful for your help. But are you guys going to be able to hold yourselves in the future?" Isaac tells him "Definitely man." And describes to them their metamorphosis back home. They stock up on meat and during full moons survive off of that, and hunt wild animals in the woods as a pack. In this way they have managed to keep the peace in their community living side by side. The whole pack has adapted to the change and have their own lifestyle. Paul agrees exclaiming, "We've been doing this successfully for a really long time before Isaac came to us." Sam is happy to hear it because it's an awkward position to be in, since they would have already taken Paul's pack out if it had not been for their friendship with Isaac. Nonetheless he thanks them for they help.

Next they decide to take Isaac and Paul back to their car so that they can get back to their pack. They drive through the woods and back to the town's entrance. Isaac goes to the trunk and grabs some proper clothes for him and Paul. Then they excuse themselves for a bit behind a nearby bush to dress. Once presentable they are happy to be in warm clothes, and walk back over to the brothers. Duke tells them to take care and thanks them for coming thorough for them. They shake hands and he orders them to get some rest since they had a bad fall. Sam adds, "We are truly grateful and couldn't have done it without you and Paul." They agree to take a little rest and assures them they're fine, just a little bruised. Likewise Isaac adds, "I am happy to be a team once again, it was an adventure and a pleasure." They exchange goodbyes, high fives and climb into their car, honking as they turn out. Duke turns to Sam and says, "You know what after all that, I feel hungry let's go back and get something to eat, my treat!" Sam laughs.

They drive back to the local diner and grab something to eat. It's not too crowded and many of the customers recognize them as the agents that helped save the town. The patrons smile and gesture. The waiter is cheerful and takes their order, today they both agree on cheeseburgers, fries and a soda. After the waiter leaves, Duke tells Sam, "I've seen enough blood to last me a whole year!" Sam agrees with a huge sigh of relief. He also tells him that he did a great job back there and he couldn't believe the vampires speed and growth. Duke thanks his little brother and compliments his work. He says the vampire clan grew in numbers pretty fast and he was surprised when the leader explained that the vampires wanted to take the whole town for themselves. He says, "It kind of makes you wonder just how many are out there in general, and if they will try this again." The food arrives and puts a much a needed smile on both of their tired faces. Duke adds, "I am serious about you getting a normal life, you should go back to college and sit a few out. " Sam thinks about it and says it may be possible since he hasn't thought about his own personal life and dreams in years. He sort of likes the idea of starting anew and being amongst everyone else, even with all his knowledge of the supernatural. He asks Duke the same,

"Wouldn't you like to sit out a few and go on a vacation? " He smiles and reminds him that he played a pretty good coach back at the old high school! Duke laughs and says, "You know what, if you do it, I am game, why not?! We deserve a little change and these ghouls and vampires just keep coming, so we can take our pick." They discuss it more over their meal. Then Duke looks up and notices Doctor Hudson prettily walking in very cheerfully. She recognizes them and walks over to the table to say hello. They greet her warmly noticing the sweet smell of jasmine that lingers with her, Duke tries to avoid staring too hard. She thanks them for the antidote for the officers. And explains, "That it worked really well, their vitals look great and they appear to be getting better. You know if the agent thing doesn't work out you guys might want to try science." She hands Duke a business card, smiles and says, "It was the strangest rabies case I've ever seen, and then how about those maniacs on the loose, all of the mania made me feel like I was in the city again."

She mentions the town has a tendency to have a routine way of life and whenever anything out of the ordinary happens everyone makes a big deal out of it. Duke "Says I am glad we could help, it's our job." Sam adds that sometimes routine can be a good thing, and tells her that they like the town. Doctor Hudson then asks, "Are you guys sticking around for a few days?" She mentions since things have calmed down, they should take some time to see the town's beauty. It has lots of outdoor activities and is really peaceful. Duke looks at the card and puts it in his pocket, then surprises Sam when he says, "You know we'll probably stay a few days.

7

One for the Road

Maybe you could show us around?" Doctor Hudson
replies, "Sure, my uncle who knows every spot here
just give us a call." She then tells them she has to
pick up her order at the counter, and then invites
them to a community BBQ at the lake at 3:00 pm,
adding, "You guys are more than welcome to attend
and the whole community would love to thank the
both of you for all of your help." Duke smiles and
says, "Okay, we'll meet you at the lake, see you
later." The waiter behind the counter tells the
Doctor her order is ready, so she excuses herself
and tells them she will see them later. They wave to
her as she leaves.

Sam is surprised and wonders what changed
his mind into staying so quickly. He smiles, and
Duke says "Everyone's pretty nice here and we are
going to the BBQ and getting the tour!" Sam laughs
and says, "All is back to normal." They finish up
their meal the waiter tells them everything was on
the house, so Sam thanks him and leaves a really
good tip. Both feel things maybe looking up for
them. They leave and drive back to the hotel to
freshen up for the barbeque. They are feeling happy
and spruce up more than usual. Sam asks Duke
about his sudden change of heart. Duke says, "The
town feels good and I'd like to stick around and
may be meet a few people." Sam smiles because he
thinks people mean the Doctor but time will tell. He

says, "It's time to go." And suggest they stop by the grocery store to bring chips and dip. Duke loves the idea and seems like a perfectly normal thing to do! After picking up the snacks they meet up with Doctor Hudson, her uncle along with many of the neighbors at the lake. The weather is perfect and the sun is low, everything is lit up with candles and lanterns. There are soft cushiony spots for everyone to relax and eat. Sam asks to help at the grill and Doctor Hudson's uncle Ali is happy to get some help. He thanks Sam for his work and says the FBI's lucky to have them. Meanwhile Duke talks with Dr. Hudson, while everyone's having a good time. Duke sets a meet-up with Uncle Ali and Dr. Hudson for a tour, as promised. The next day they see the beauty of the town, visit the local historical museum and look at many artifacts dating back to the 1700s. Later they go out for dinner and few games of pool. Overall it was the most relaxing couple of days the brothers have had in years. But soon they receive a call with a new lead to follow. The new life will have to wait. They pile up everything and drive off in their Skylark on to the next case.

Author's Note

Thank you for reading and I hope it was fun! It's was a lot fun writing this story, because I am such a fan of horror stories. And writing one gave me a chance to bring something spooky to the arena. Also I enjoyed sharing it with so many of you. Look out for more short stories, and keep in touch via the net at www.missaishaharris.blogspot.com.

All the best,

Aisha Harris

Fright Night. Copyright © 2015 by Aisha Harris. All rights reserved.